MONA the VAMPIRE

MEN IN DARK

Dear Reader,
Watch out for the pictures with wibbly-wobbly edges –
you will be entering the Mona Zone!

SCHOLASTIC CANADA LTD.

One morning, Mona's class was just finishing a math test.
"Mona," said Miss Gotto. "Please would you, Lily and Charley,
go over to the audiovisual department and get the slide projector?"
"Come on," said Mona, and Charley and Lily raced for the door.

"Before I forget, class," announced Miss Gotto as the door closed behind them, "St. Faith's will have some special visitors today."

Out in the hallway, Mona spotted something that made them stop running – a strange black car was parked in front of the school.

Then Mona heard strange voices down the hall. She peeped around the corner and saw two peculiar men in dark suits.

"The General will find no obstacles," said one of the men. "It'll be another victory for the UN."

"The United Nations?" asked Charley. "No," Mona gasped. "Uranus Nexeerians – aliens! I'd recognize them anywhere! They brainwash earthlings, then take them back to their home planet to work in their salt mines."

Mona, Charley and Lily had to warn everyone! They rushed back to the classroom and burst through the door.

"What took so long, Mona?" asked Miss Gotto crossly. "And where is the slide projector?"

"I don't want to cause a panic, but . . ." Mona gulped, ". . . the UN are coming!"

"We know," said Miss Gotto impatiently.

"We know, we know," chanted the class.

"Uh-oh! They're already brainwashed," thought Mona.

In the cafeteria, Lily looked around nervously.

"I can't tell who is brainwashed and who's not," she said.

"The ears!" said Mona. "Clean ears, washed brain."

Suddenly the Men in Dark Suits joined the line-up at the counter.

"Act naturally," hissed Charley.

Phooosh!

Mona, Charley and Lily dove under the table just in time. They watched in horror as the two hideous aliens brainwashed everyone in the cafeteria with a blast from their strange, green eyes.

"What are we going to do?" asked Lily after they had escaped. "The interesting thing about Nexeerians is that they're easy to brainwash," said Mona thoughtfully. "I have a plan – let's go and find that slide projector. This is a job for Mona the Vampire!"

In the audiovisual department, they found a strobe light and a stopwatch. The friends went back into the hall and they set their trap.

"Go back to your own planet – we're still using ours," chanted Mona, as the strobe flashed on and off spookily.

Then Mona popped up with the borrowed watch.

"You are getting sleepy, sleeeepy . . ." droned Mona. "You want to go home to your own universe."

"That's it," said one of the agents. "I'm going back to my own planet!"

Later, in Principal Shawbly's office, Mona tried in
vain to explain the situation but the Principal was furious.
"I've had complaints from our guests from the UN. Apparently you
tried to hypnotize one of them and made him think he was an alien!
All we ask is for you kids to stay out of the way," yelled the Principal.

Just then, the school secretary put her head around the door.
"General Harundi from the UN has arrived."
The Principal hurried out and the three friends rushed to see.
"Oh no!" gulped Charley as they looked at the scene outside.

The General got out of his car and stared up at the window. "Uh-oh!" shrieked Mona, as he changed into a hideous alien.

Later, as Principal Shawbly showed the General around St. Faith's, Angela pushed in front of them and curtsied.

"My name is Angela. I have been rightfully chosen to present you with a book today," she simpered.

The Men in Dark Suits moved Angela to one side as she chattered on about herself, and the group hurried away.

The Mayor was due to present the key of the city to the General.

"Oh no!" whispered Mona. "If the General has the key, the Uranus Nexeerians will have access to the whole town's brain supply!"

"Not if we stop him first," said Lily.

"Doing that will require quick thinking and skill — and we've got to get Angela out of the way," said Mona.

"Hey, look at that beautiful dress, Angela!" Mona gasped, as she pushed Angela into their classroom and locked the door behind her.

"Now for my disguise," said Mona happily as she ran off down the hallway.

Meanwhile, at City Hall, the Mayor had begun to panic. The stage
for the presentation to the General was still being finished.

"The UN will be here any second," moaned the Mayor. "Hurry up!"

"On behalf of the city, I welcome you, General Harundi," announced the Mayor, still on edge.

The wobbly stage creaked and shook as the Men in Dark Suits stepped onto the platform.

"From St. Faith's School to present a gift to the General..." the Mayor continued, "...Angela Smith!"

Mona walked onto the stage in her Angela disguise and graciously handed the book to General Harundi, who was squinting suspiciously at her.

"Umm, did I tell you I got an award for being me?" Mona simpered in her Angela voice.

"Hey, it's the vampire girl who hypnotized me!" hissed one of the UN agents. "We've got to get her out of there; she's going to ruin everything."

The agents closed in and hurried Mona off the stage.
"Hey, what's going on?" cried Mona, struggling to get away.

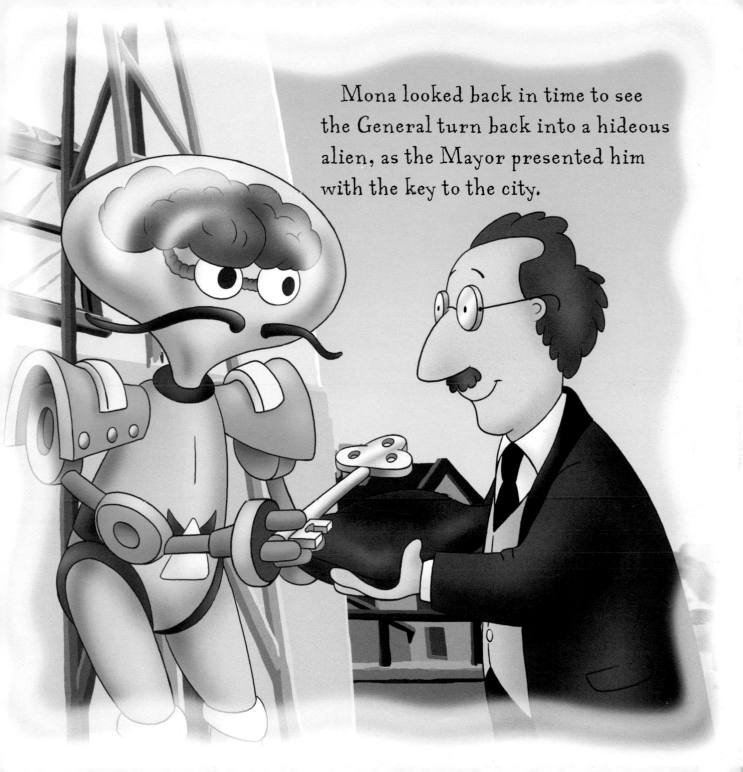

Mona looked back in time to see the General turn back into a hideous alien, as the Mayor presented him with the key to the city.

At last Mona struggled free. She hurled herself towards the stage.
She couldn't let the Uranus Nexeerian General have that key!

Mona grabbed the key, and the
General and the Mayor stumbled
backward off the stage. The boards
and supports wobbled and creaked...

. . . and the shaky stage collapsed into a heap behind them. As Mona gazed at the wreck, the angry Mayor hurried over to her.

"Do you realize what you have done?" said the Mayor, fuming.

Just then, a gentle hand landed on Mona's shoulder. It was one of the Men in Dark Suits. He was smiling.

"She's just saved General Harundi's life. That stage was about to collapse on him — this young lady is a hero!"

"Umm, congratulations!" mumbled the Mayor.

Later, Mona and her friends were in a crowd gathered to say goodbye to the General.

"I owe you a big favour," said the General. "How can I repay you?"

"Simple," replied Mona, blushing a little. "Instead of invading Earth, I want you to protect it."

At bedtime, Mona looked at the front page of the paper.
"Little girl saves UN Secretary-General," she read proudly.
"Well, Fang, we can all sleep safer tonight."